RICH STRYKER PI:
Julie's Last Hope

Tamara L Adams

RICH STRYKER: Julie's Last Hope

This book is a work of fiction. Names, characters, businesses, organiza- tions, places, events and incidents either are the product of the author's imagination or are used fictitiously. Any resemblance to actual persons, living or dead, events, or locales is entirely coincidental.

For information contact :

http://www.tamaraladamsauthor.com[1]

tamaraadamsauthor@gmail.com

Pleases consider leaving a review ! It is your greatest compliment !

Book and Cover design by Tamara using Canva

Chapter One

It's a hot one today. Over a hundred degrees with a shirt-soaking humidity.

It's the kind of day that brings out the crazy of Chicago. People get irritated and start committing stupid crimes. But I guess it is not my problem anymore now that I'm retired from the force.

Though it doesn't keep me from worrying about the innocent people on the streets who eventually come to me for help when the police drop the ball.

Amanda interrupts my thoughts. "Rich, you have a Mr. Nelson here to see you."

I have no recollection of a Mr. Nelson or any scheduled appointments, but business is slow. "Alright, send him in."

A few seconds later the door opens and in walks an older gentleman with bloodshot eyes and disheveled hair. "Thank you for taking the time to see me Mr. Stryker." He reaches out a hand.

I stand up and shake it. "No problem. What can I help you with, Mr. Nelson?"

"Carl, call me Carl."

"Okay, Carl, what seems to be the issue?"

"Well, sir, I'm not sure what kind of cases you take, but my granddaughter has been missing since Friday. My daughter is worried sick and the police seem to think she is just another teenage runaway. But we know better, sir. My wife recalled your mother talking about her detective son, so we asked for your office address. I hope you don't mind me dropping by like this, but we didn't know where else to turn. No one else will help."

"No problem at all, Carl. I'm here to help, and any friend of my mother is a friend of mine."

"Thank you, sir! You don't know how much this means to us."

"You can call me Rich, and don't thank me yet. First let's see if I can help. How about you tell me everything that has happened so far? Give it to me straight and don't leave anything out. The truth will get me farther than any sugarcoating, okay?"

"You got it, sir. I mean Rich. Thank you."

Carl spends the next hour telling me about his grandchild. A sixteen-year-old girl named Julie. She had always been a good kid, got good grades and obeyed the rules.

Recently, she'd gotten involved with a group of kids of whom Carl was not a fan. There were rumors going around about the kids selling drugs, and no matter how much Carl and his wife, Glenda, pleaded their case, Julie wouldn't listen. Florence, Carl's daughter, also suspected Julie was seeing one of the boys in the group.

Friday Julie asked to sleep over at Emily's house, but Florence had said no. Emily was a new friend, and Julie had been giving Florence attitude all week. The two argued before Julie stormed out.

When Julie did not return home that night, Florence thought her daughter had just disobeyed her and stayed overnight anyway.

Then Saturday night came around and Julie still hadn't come home or called, so Florence began to worry. She called everyone she knew, but no one had seen Julie since Friday and she never did stay over at Emily's house that Friday night.

Florence called the police who were convinced it's a teenage runaway case. They claimed they would look into it, but Florence hadn't heard anything since.

Florence and her parents had done everything they could think of to find Julie but had come up with no leads. The family was at their wits end and that is when Glenda remembered Linda talking about her detective son.

Now I'm their last hope.

I have never taken on a missing person case, not even during my time on the force. I had always worked homicide, so this would be a whole new ball game for me, and I'm not certain I want to play.

I stare Carl in the eye. I need the truth. "You're certain she has not run away? You did say she and her mother had been fighting the day she went missing."

"Rich, I'm certain, more certain than anything else right now. Julie is a typical moody teenager, but not the kind to just leave. She is a good kid. She may have had a few issues here and there, but what teenager doesn't? We need your help here. We need it bad. I fear the worst." His eyes plead with me.

"Alright, I'll ask around and find some things out. We'll go from there. I'll get a sense for what's going on and get back to you, okay?"

"Thank you so much. You don't know how much this means to us. And I promise we will get you the down payment soon."

"How about we not worry till later about the money, okay? For now I will need you to get a list together of all Julie's friends with numbers and addresses, plus any info you can get to me on her recent hangouts. Sometimes the friends know more than you think. Give me it all and I'll work my way through it before we talk money. Okay, Carl?"

"Okay, I'll get you everything. Thank you so much."

Carl leaves after what seems like an eternity of 'thank yous.' It was exhausting, and brought on more pressure to solve the case. What have I got myself into? This will not be easy.

"Amanda, can you come in here a minute?"

"Sure, boss."

I cringe at the word boss. No matter how many times I tell her to stop, she still calls me that.

"Please Amanda, call me Rich."

"Sorry. What do you need...Rich?"

"I need you to find any recent missing teen reports to get a heads-up on them for this one."

"Missing person, huh? This is a new one. I'll get on it, boss." She spins around to leave and I spot her six-inch platform shoes and tight mini-skirt.

I roll my eyes. She is a piece of work and the flashiest assistant I've ever seen. When I offered her the job I told her the dress code, but apparently her idea of business casual is different than the rest of the world. No amount of castigation from me will change it.

I have to remind myself Amanda is one of the best assistants I have ever worked with, including on the force. You can count on her to do the research, track down a lead, or find any kind of source you want.

I learned long ago not to ask too many questions on how she comes up with some of the info. She's also the only person I've met that has a photographic memory. It amazes me she never used the gift for much good before I came along.

But that's what happens when you grow up with an abusive father and drug addict mother. Amanda was hooking before she was sixteen and addicted to every kind of drug by nineteen.

The girl had been through hell and back before ending up in a cell one night while I was on duty. She witnessed a triple homicide when a client turned crazy. Her memory and description of the scene caught my attention.

Intrigued by her unique talent, I knew I had to help her. After much convincing, I made a deal with her; I would pay for her to get cleaned up and give her a place to stay if she worked for the force as an informant. She was not too keen on the idea, but getting a place of her own and not having to sleep with random men every night was enticing enough for her to give it a try.

Now here we are, two years later. She stopped being an informant a few months after I left the force and came to work for me. We make a great team. I'm the brains and brawn, and she has a talent for acquiring information.

Business is decent enough for me to pay myself and give Amanda a generous salary, while still being able to supplement my mother if need be. With so much corruption on the police force, the neighborhood needed another place to turn when times get tough.

I'm that place and it feels good to make a difference. The cops don't like me meddling in their business, but I couldn't care less what they do or do not like. Most of them still dislike why I left, and the feeling is mutual for a majority of the force.

Though my old friend Anderson is an exception. He is one guy I can count on to never be corrupt. Even the bad cops can't help but like him. It broke his heart to watch me leave the force, but we still keep in contact. He helps me out once in a while, and in return I do things he can't or won't to get answers. It's a win-win.

Today I need his help. I pick up the phone and hope he's at his desk.

Chapter Two

I'm in luck. "Anderson speaking."

"Hey, old buddy. How you been?"

"Hey, Rich. I'm good. It's been a while. How are things? How's your mom?"

"Things are good, and she's doing well. Is the precinct treating you well these days?"

"It is. Things are good. So, what can I help you with, Rich?"

"Well, I have a new case, a missing girl."

"Really? That's a new one."

"Yeah. I almost didn't accept the case, but when they told me the officer assigned, I had to take it."

"Do I even want to know?"

"Maybe not, but here it goes. Officer Benny Hartman thinks the girl is a runaway, not missing. The family disagrees whole-heartedly, and so far I believe them. I'm not sure dear old Benny boy is going to do a good enough job of looking into the case, if you know what I mean."

"I fear you may be right on this one, Rich. What is it you need from me?"

"I was hoping to get all the details you can dig up on any recent missing girl cases in the area. If I can find a connection between them and my girl, I may have a chance of getting somewhere."

"I'll see what I can find and get back to you."

"Thanks, John. I owe you one."

The phone clicks and I decide to head to Debbie's Diner down the block for lunch. Amanda's on the phone at her desk when I leave my office.

"Hold on a sec." She covers the receiver.

"I'm headed to Debbie's. Want me to wait so you can join me?"

"Nah. I'm onto something."

"I'll bring you back a burger and fries."

She winks at me. "Thanks, boss."

It's as hot as a sauna outside and I almost turn around to go back into air conditioning, but I already have my heart set on a double cheeseburger, so I power through the heat till I reach the diner.

Once inside, air hits me like a blast of Arctic wind, and I'm instantly refreshed.

Corrine, my usual waitress, waves as I sit down at the counter. "Hey, Sugar, what can I get you?"

"Hello, Corrine. Today I'll take the double cheeseburger with a side of onion rings."

"Sure thing, Sugar. Want your Mt. Dew to go with that, honey?"

"You know me too well. I would love one. Thank you."

She saunters off to put in my order.

I search around the diner, spotting most of the lunch regulars, as well as a few new faces. This place has been a favorite of mine since my early days on the force, ten years ago.

My partner and I had investigated Debbie's robbery, and she offered us a meal. I've been hooked ever since. Finding an office within walking distance for my private firm was a huge reason for me choosing to buy the place I'm at now.

The place come as a fixer-upper, and I spent weeks cleaning and repainting to make it presentable. The old plumbing turned into my nemesis and I nearly gave up, but eventually it all came together.

This place is worth the pain. Debbie makes the best burgers I've ever tasted and I now am an addict. These burgers and my Mt. Dew will be the death of me, but it's so worth it. They are my vice – them and Twinkies. There is always a box of those in my right bottom drawer. I reach for one anytime I'm in my office and stressed.

The way I eat, you'd expect me to be plagued with heart disease or diabetes, but I keep fit with karate, which also comes in handy in some tight situations.

I may not be the biggest or the strongest guy, but my five-foot-six frame, holding one hundred forty pounds, surprises people when I can hold my own in a fight. Karate can teach you a thing or two.

Laughter draws my attention to the corner booth which holds a group of teenagers. Julie pops into my mind and I wonder why the heck I said I'd take the case.

This isn't the first time my proud mother sent me a tough case, due to her bragging, but it certainly is the most difficult. No matter how many times I tell her my job is no big deal, she still insists on telling everyone she knows 'My son's a big private investigator. Yep, solves every case he gets. He can help anyone.'

It's not all true, but she won't listen to me on that either. Mothers and their love. I'll never complain, but at times it can be a bit much.

"Here you go, Sugar – your burger, onion rings and soda. Can I getcha anything else, honey?"

"Nope. I'm good for now, but I will take an order to go later."

"Anything for you, Sugar." She heads off to help a customer while I dig in.

It's heaven in my mouth, juicy and exploding with flavor. Even the onion rings are delicious beyond description. I swear Debbie fries these in crack, but I'm not complaining.

Chapter Three

The meal has me in a trance and I don't notice anyone beside me until she speaks. "Good, huh?"

Caught in the middle of a bite, I choke on my burger before I get it down. "Delicious."

She puts out a hand. "My name is Victoria. I'm new to the place. Is there anything you recommend?"

"My favorite is the double cheeseburger and onion rings, but to be honest everything on the menu is amazing, so you can't choose wrong."

"Really?"

"Yep, I've been eating here for years and have never had anything I didn't like."

"Thanks."

"No problem." The burger draws me in for another bite.

"Do you work nearby?"

I finish chewing. "Yep, a few blocks up."

"Oh, nice. It seems like a real nice area."

"Yep."

"What is it you do, Mr...?"

The burger calls my name and onion rings never taste as good cold, but I turn to her. "Rich Stryker. I'm a private investigator."

Her eyes light up. "Oh, how exciting!"

Just then, I notice her beautiful blue eyes and long wavy brown hair, which hugs her face.

"What types of crimes do you investigate?" Her smile beams her excitement.

"Oh, thefts, cheating spouses, and money laundering. The usual you would expect from a private eye. But I've recently taken a missing person's case, so my life is about to get a little less boring. A local teenage girl." I'm not sure why I'm telling her about the case. Arrogance was never one of my characteristics, but she is wearing a low cut v-neck t-shirt and her large perky breasts are interrupting my reasonable thinking.

"Well, I hope you find the poor girl."

"I'm confident I'll find her. It's only a matter of time." There I go again. I might as well stand up and beat my chest while yelling 'me smart, strong man, me save the day.' My cheeks have to be red hot by now but Victoria seems to not notice.

"Oh, well, that's good. You must be a terrific investigator if families trust you with finding their daughters."

Trying not to ooze douchey pride, I take a deep breath. "I do a good enough job to please my clients. I mean I've had no issues yet, anyway." At least those are true words.

"I bet you're just being modest Mr. Stryker." She pats my arm and I wonder if she's flirting with me.

No, she can't be I decide. She is a good looking woman – on the petite side, with a soft button nose, high cheek bones, and pouty lips.

Why would she flirt with me? I'm an average-looking man. Some would even put me on the nerdy side of the aisle.

"Rich, call me Rich."

She flashes me a gorgeous smile. "Rich, I like that name."

"What is it that you do, Victoria?"

"I'm a psychology professor at The University of Chicago."

"Fascinating, I've always been interested in human behavior. How long have you been teaching there?"

"I've only been there two weeks. I just moved from Whitewater, Wisconsin. I haven't started teaching yet, since it's summer and all, but I'm preparing my syllabus and getting ready for the fall semester."

"I'm sure you'll be an amazing instructor." I wonder if she just graduated from college. Early twenties is a bit young for my tastes, since I'm thirty-three. She does look like twenty-two could be a possibility. "Did you teach back at Whitewater?"

"I was an assistant professor there for six years after my education in the psych department. I loved it there, but this job was too good to pass up."

"I don't know much about Wisconsin, but Chicago is a great city. Lots to do and great people. I think you'll like it here."

"I already do, but I don't know many people here. I want to experience it all but exploring the city alone seems scary."

"I can understand how a large, busy city would be a lot to take in. You'll just have to find someone to explore it with you."

Her smile fades a little. "True. I could ask a co-worker, but most of them are married and have kids already and are too busy."

"Oh."

We sit there in silence for a minute. My burger screams my name, but her beauty diverts all my attention.

"Would you excuse me for a moment?" she asks.

"Sure."

She gets up and heads to the restroom, lean calves stretching out from her knee-length skirt.

"Oh, you wouldn't know flirting if it hit you on the ass, sweetheart." Corrine smiles at me from behind the counter.

"What?"

"Sugar, that woman is flirting with you. She is trying to get you to ask her out, or at least show her around the city, but you're too oblivious to see it. Wake up, Sugar, ask her out." Corrine laughs. "Did you want to give me that order for Amanda now? The usual?"

"Um......yes. Thanks, Corrine."

She continues to laugh as she walks off to help a customer.

I've been clueless about women my whole life, so my mishandling of Victoria comes as no surprise, and I still am not sure how to handle it.

I take the chance to finish my burger and onion rings while they are still warm. The last onion ring goes down as I spot her walking back to her seat.

"Have you decided what to order?"

"I think I'll try the cheeseburger and onion rings. Yours look good. Maybe I'll live a little and get a root beer float."

"Excellent choice."

She smiles at me and now I feel an awkward silence between us. "Um...about Chicago. I may have time to show you around Jackson Park and the waterfront. It has a beautiful garden and sculptures throughout. That is, if you'd like."

The bright smile returns to her face. "That would be terrific. Thank you!"

"Can I pick you up around five-thirty?"

"Sounds great. I'll be leaving work, so you could meet me in front of the Harper Memorial Library. Does that work?"

"That'll work."

"Here you go, Sugar."

I hand Corrine a twenty and a ten. "Keep the change, Corrine."

"Thanks, Sugar. You tell Amanda I say hi."

Victoria gives me a confused look and it takes me a moment to realize she wonders who Amanda is, but she is too nice to ask.

"I'm bringing lunch back for my assistant. She's a workaholic sometimes and didn't want to leave the office today."

Her face relaxes. "That's so nice of you. Thanks for keeping me company."

"Sure thing. I'll see you at five-thirty."

"See you then."

Thoughts of Victoria fill my mind on the walk back to the office. What should I show her? The Statue of the Republic may be the best place to start, and then move on from there.

Amanda is still on the phone when I get back. I put her food on the desk. She waves and mouths 'thank you'.

The task of finding Julie looms over me, so I head to my office not knowing where to start. I decide to begin with my usual ritual of filling out index cards on everyone surrounding the case –

Carl and his wife, the mother and her argument with Julie, the suspected boyfriend and friends, even one on Officer Benny Hartman, not one of my favorites from the force. The guy is arrogant, and I suspect he beat every girlfriend he ever had.

Next I fill out cards with every detail involved in the case and tape them all up on the huge dry erase board hung up along the left wall of my office. It's the typical image you see on any cop show, but laying out the whole case really does help you put together the pieces of the puzzle.

I'm studying the board when Amanda bursts into my office. She is never one to knock.

"You're never gonna believe this, Rich. I made some calls and found out that there have been multiple missing teen cases around the South Side. Some of them have been reported, but plenty of others were assumed runaways or the parents didn't care enough to worry." She paces around the room. "Those poor girls. Who knows what's happened to them. We have to figure this one out, Rich. I need you to solve this case and fast. We can't have all these poor girls being plucked from the streets for who knows what. One of my friends suggests reasons for their being kidnapped that I don't want to think about. Do you know how awful people can be out there?"

She does not wait for a response. "Well I do and I am not gonna let those girls go through that. No siree. Here are a few printouts of the reported cases, and I'm gonna type up the rest of my notes on the unreported ones to send to you." She hands me the stack of papers.

Pictures of girls are at the top of each and a write-up below of what the parents told the police about their missing daughters. It breaks my heart to see their young faces looking back at me. "We've got this, Amanda. Don't you worry. We will figure this one out. I won't let you or the Nelsons down."

"I know you won't." She heads for the door. "Thanks for the food, boss." She leaves before I can respond.

I head back to my desk and fill out cards for each of the other missing girls.

Chapter Four

Ages of the girls range from twelve to seventeen, and the stories resemble each other. Young girls from single-parent or poor homes, spending too much time hanging out with friends for their families to think too much about their absence until it's too late.

None of them found.

These cases are probably assigned to cops too busy to really dig into them. From what I know of missing person's reports, there is usually not enough evidence to work up a clear conclusion as to what happened.

Amanda's stricken face comes to mind and I tell myself to figure it out. I have to figure this out.

My computer pings and I find Amanda's email with notes about the other missing girls – ones never reported to the police.

These cases are less detailed, and darker – stories of girls from abusive homes, running around on the streets at a young age. They are in and out of trouble for years, and then they disappear, and no one hears from them. The parents either assume they've run away or couldn't care less where they've gone. All they know is it's one less mouth to feed.

Writing out cards for these girls is harder, and I find myself rushing to get them done. It sickens me to learn how some children are treated. Part of me itches to go and show the parents a taste of their own disturbing medicine. I open my desk drawer and pull out a Twinkie, needing something to calm me down.

Amanda pushes open my door. "I'm gonna head out a bit early today, boss. I've got a lead and I need to talk to them now. Ugh, how can you eat those things?"

"These…" I raise the Twinkie, "are delicious. I'll see you tomorrow."

"Way too much sugar." She shakes her head. "Bye, Rich."

I'm almost too stunned by her use of my first name to respond. "Amanda?"

She stops.

"Take care of yourself out there."

She smiles. "You worry too much, boss." And leaves.

The clock reads four-thirty. I decide to tape all the cards of the other missing girls up on the board in an order that makes sense to me at the moment. I can look at it with fresh eyes in the morning. I organize them by where they live, for lack of better options.

There are too many cases for it to be a matter of all runaways. What happened to all these girls? So far there were twenty-three, twenty-four counting Julie. Something has to be going on, and I am going to get to the bottom of it. But for now I have to head out and meet Victoria.

The school is about fifteen blocks away so even though it's blistering hot I decide to walk. As I get closer, I spot a street vendor selling coffee. I order two iced lattes and walk up to the library with a few minutes to spare. I plop down on a bench, my mind still on the missing girls.

"Rich, have you been waiting long?" Victoria's voice shakes me out of my thoughts.

"Nope, I just got here." I hand her one of the drinks. "I brought you a latte."

She flashes a killer smile. "Thanks. This will be nice. It's a hot one out here."

"It is. Would you rather do something inside?"

"No, it'll be okay. I've been wanting to visit the park for a while now, and who knows when this heat will die down."

"Sounds good. It's only a few blocks away. Did you want to walk or grab a cab?"

"I'm up for a walk if you are."

"Sure thing."

We head east in silence. I've never been much of a talker.

"Have you lived in the city your whole life?"

"Yep. I grew up on the South Side. My mom still lives in our old house about twenty-five blocks southwest of here. I moved closer to work, and rent an apartment about fifteen blocks south of Debbie's Diner."

"That burger was delicious, by the way. I may have to make that place a regular stop."

"It's the best place to eat in town, that's for sure."

"I'll have to get your take on the best pizza place in town for that deep-dish Chicago pizza I hear all about."

"Oh, there is a great deep-dish pizza place, Al's Pizza, about five blocks west of the park. We could go there afterward if you'd like."

"I would. Thanks!"

The park isn't too busy, since it's a Monday and hot out like an oven, but there are still plenty of people around the statue when we arrive.

"It's prettier in person than the pictures I've seen." Victoria studies it intently.

"It's a great piece of art – one of my favorites in the city."

We admire the statue, gold and glittering in the sun, and then a young boy bumps into Victoria, pushing her forward.

"Sorry ma'am." He moves on.

Reacting quickly I grab his hand. "Give it back."

"What do you mean, sir?"

"You know perfectly well what I mean. Give the lady her wallet back."

"I don't have it, sir."

"Rich, please, what are you doing? He's just a boy."

"Victoria, would you do me a favor and check your purse. Make sure you still have your wallet."

"Rich I'm sure it was an accident. Please let him go."

"I will as soon as you check for your wallet."

"Okay." She digs into her purse and pauses to look at me, then opens it up wide, moving its contents around a few times before looking up at me. "It's not here."

I turn to the dirty-haired boy, clothes a little on the small side. "Give it back and I won't call the cops."

"Okay, okay." The kid pulls out the wallet from his pocket and hands it to Victoria.

"Tell the lady you're sorry."

The kid looks at his shoes.

"Tell her!"

"Sorry ma'am."

"Oh, it's okay." Victoria's smiles in sympathy.

"I'm disappointed you are pick-pocketing strangers, and I hope you learn to put those quick hand skills to good work doing something else, like magic on the corner or who knows what. I'm going to give you this." I slowly release his hand, hoping he won't run, and reach for my pocket. "Here's my card. If you ever need help or want to do some honest work, you give me a call. And here..." I write down the address to a nearby shelter. "This is a shelter you can go to for a bed and food. Now, here's a ten. Go get yourself some food and leave these people alone, okay?"

The kid stares at me.

"Life is tough, kid, and street life is even harder, but crime is not the answer and there are people that want to help you, so please go to the shelter if you need it or call me, okay?"

"Okay." It's all I get before he takes off down the street, but it's enough.

I turn to find Victoria staring at me.

"How did you know? I felt nothing to make me think he took anything."

"You live here long enough, you see everything and learn to notice when something's not right."

"And instead of getting mad, you gave him money and a place to go for help. That was truly great of you, Rich. You're a wonderful, giving man." She gives me a peck on the cheek.

My face turns bright red, and I attempt to turn the attention away from me. "Did you want to walk around and check out the other art and the garden?"

"Yes I would." She grabs my hand.

Along the way I learn Victoria grew up in the tiny town of Emerald Grove, twenty miles from Whitewater. She did her post-doctoral work at Whitewater before getting an assistant professor position. She stayed there until her big move to the Windy City. This is the farthest she has ever been from home other than a few trips to Milwaukee's fairs and entertainment.

I can relate a little bit. I had only really left my little part of the world to attend the police academy before heading straight back to work on the force. It's hard to leave home, especially when you have a great childhood with two loving parents, as Victoria had.

We move throughout the park checking out all the sculptures and the spectacular garden. Victoria's favorite is the koi pond, so we sit awhile and watch the fish swim around. There is plenty of shade and a breeze coming off the water. The silence is comfortable, unlike our silence at the diner earlier. I turn and smile at her. "I'm hungry. Still up for that pizza?"

"I sure am. Let's go."

Chapter Five

Victoria's enthralled with the tall city buildings. She's not used to all the fast-food restaurants and shopping centers on the lower floors with several flights of stairs worth of apartment and office buildings above them. To her it is crazy for so much to be crammed into such a small plot of land.

At Al's, they seat us right away and we order a chicken, pepper, mushroom, and white sauce deep dish-pizza.

"So how did you come to be a private investigator, Rich?"

"It's a long story."

"We have time, if you don't mind sharing."

"Well I'll give you the shorter version for now. I had wanted to be a police officer from a young age, so when I turned eighteen I attended the police academy, then graduated and joined the Chicago PD right out of training. I loved being a police officer and worked hard to keep the city of Chicago a safe place to live. Before too long I realized the corruption within the city, and it shocked me to see so many of my fellow officers in the thick of it." I stop to drink some water.

Victoria's face shows concern.

"I tried for years to pull some of my colleagues out of the life, but the greed and blackmail from the city criminals was too much for them to overcome. Eventually I gave up and left the force. I still wanted to help the people of the city, so I started my own private eye business, and now here I am."

"That's quite a story, Rich. Someday I would like to hear more." Her cheeks flush red. "I mean, you know, if you'd like to show me more of the city sometime."

"I would like that. There's a lot more to see."

Our pizza arrives, so we dig in.

"Oh..yum....this is delicious, Rich. Thanks for taking me here."

"I'm glad you like it."

We talk more about her teaching position and the places in Chicago she'd like to visit in between bites of pizza. By the time we finish, it is after eight and a tad more tolerable outside.

"Did you want me to walk you home?"

"I appreciate it. Thank you."

"Which way do you live?"

"I only live about five blocks south of here, I think." She grabs my hand and smiles. "Is that out of your way?"

"Nope. I'm on my way to my mother's, and your place is in the same direction."

"You're a sweet man, going to check on your mom."

"I'm all she has, and if I don't check in every night in some shape or form she worries. Always has."

"You're her baby boy. She'll always worry. Your dad's no longer around?"

"He hasn't been around for a while. He left us when I was young and we haven't heard from him since. We were probably better off without him. My mom is a strong woman, and we had a good life."

"Being a single mom does take strength, especially thirty years ago. I applaud her."

I'm not ready to delve into the rest of my past, so I point out interesting scenic buildings and stores Veronica may want to visit as we walk.

Conversation with her comes more naturally than with most, and she even appreciates my dry humor. In no time, we arrive at her apartment building.

"Thanks for showing me around and taking me to that amazing pizza place."

"It was my pleasure. Would you like me to show you around some more, another time?"

"I would like that very much."

I pull out my cell phone. "If you give me your number I'll call you to set up another time to meet."

I type in her number and put the phone away, realizing the uncomfortable moment has come. Do I shake her hand? Give her a hug? I probably don't go in for a kiss, do I?

"Well, thanks again."

She gives me a look I, of course, can't read for crap, so I play the safest route and stick out my hand. "It was great to meet you and even better to spend time with you. I'll call soon."

"Great to meet you too, and I would like that."

We shake for longer than what seems normal then she releases my hand.

"Goodnight, Rich."

"Good night, Victoria."

I watch her walk up the stairs to make sure she makes it safely inside then turn around and hurry to my mothers. She's probably waiting to hear from me.

I REACH HER HOUSE TO find her watching TV and eating her usual strawberry shortcake and vanilla ice cream in the living room.

"Hey mom."

"Hello, sweetie. I was starting to worry when you didn't call or stop by."

"I'm sorry, mom. The day was busy and some last minute plans came up. I'll try to remember to call next time, okay?"

"Good. I heard Mr. Nelson came by to see you. Shame about their poor missing granddaughter. You can help them, Rich. No one else believes them. They were so happy you took the case. I'm so proud of you, Rich, and all the good you do for this community. My sweet boy, always out to help others. Always have been, since the day you were born. Such a good boy."

"I'm just doing my job, mom. I'll do everything I can to find that girl."

"Oh, I just know you will find her."

It's nice my mother has such faith in me, but it may be too much. "Pre-bedtime snack, mom?"

She laughs. "We all have our vices, Rich. Sweets are mine."

"I know, mom. You passed that one on, thank you very much."

"You want one?"

"No, I'm good."

"*Castle* is about to start. You want to stay and watch?"

"Of course, wouldn't miss it."

"This week's going to be a good one. Beckett and Castle may finally hook-up, as they should've from the beginning."

"You say that every week. They will never get together, mom. It'll ruin the show."

"They will too, and no, it won't. True love never ruins anything."

I smile. Her husband leaves her with a two year old and an infant, she never marries again, and yet she still believes in true love. That's my mother, always the optimist.

It's a good episode, but still nothing happens between Beckett and Castle, though I don't point it out to my mother.

"You look tired mom. Everything okay?"

"I'm fine. It's late, so of course I'm tired. Now you go home and get some rest. You have a long day ahead of you with that Nelson case. Goodnight, sweetie."

"Goodnight, mom. I'll lock up on my way out."

"Okay, thanks."

I head out and lock the door. Then start the twelve-block trek home. Sometimes I walk away with the feeling I should move back in, to protect her. She's getting older, and the neighborhood is not the same as it used to be. It makes me worry for her safety at night. A sixty-five year-old woman is usually not equipped to take on a large twenty-something male, but she loves the house and her neighbors, so she won't move. Plus, she insists I'm too old to be living with my mother and she's too young to have her son still at home.

I laugh to myself, knowing she's right, but my worrying sometime gets the best of me. So to calm my nerves, I installed a security system in her house. She says there is no need for it, but I know it makes her feel safer and it puts my mind at ease.

You never know what to expect on the street after ten, so I keep my head high and increase my stride. There are groups of boys and young men along my walk. Some of them know me and ease off, but others stare me down, checking to see if I'm an easy target. Usually the confidence I present is enough to keep them away, but sometimes a few approach me or get up in my face, hoping to kick my ass and take my money. Even then, I stand my ground and most back down

Those who don't are sorry after laying a hand on me. My ten years of training and third-degree black belt in karate has its uses, and staying safe on the streets of Chicago at night is one of them. Now the only thugs that approach me are either high on drugs or newbies who haven't heard of me yet.

Tonight's walk is uneventful. When I get home, I think of calling Victoria to ask when she'd want to tour the city again, but decide it's too late at night to call, and probably way too soon. Aren't you supposed to wait three days to call? I shrug to myself. Dating has never been one of my strong suits, so the rules are foreign to me. I decide I'll call her tomorrow, and head to bed.

The nightmare hits me for the thousandth time. My baby sister is gone and there's nothing I can do about it.

Chapter Six

I haven't had the dream in months, and I wake in a cold sweat. Poor Kelly, taken too soon. My memories of her are fuzzy after these twenty years, but the image of her struck by that drunk driver remains vivid to this day.

This whole missing girl case must have triggered the memory, a memory I'd rather not remember.

It's only five in the morning, but I know I will not get back to sleep, so I climb out of bed and pull on some shorts and a t-shirt. The gym downstairs is open twenty-four/seven, a huge reason why I rent an apartment in this place. My work hours can get crazy, so I need the flexibility to workout.

I'm not surprised to find it empty.

The Wavemaster training bag waits for me in the far corner of the room. I put on my gloves and go at it, punching and kicking away the awful memories.

I haven't visited the dojo in a while, and wonder if I'd recognize any of the karate students anymore.

My technique still holds up to my standards, but it would most likely not be good enough for Sensei. I vow to go back soon and try to get into a regular schedule.

Next, I jump rope – not my favorite, but it's a great workout. Then I lift a few weights, still trying to pack on those last few pounds of muscle I can't seem to gain.

At six, I decide my body has had enough, so I take a shower and go out for breakfast. Jack's Pancake House sounds good right now.

Jack's is just starting to liven up when I arrive around seven.

"Watcha having today, Rich?"

"Morning, Gloria! I'm gonna have the stack of pancakes, bacon and hash browns."

"Sounds good. Did you want your Mt. Dew to go with it?"

"Ah... I shouldn't. Amanda keeps giving me crap about drinking it too much. Says no matter how fit I am, all that Dew can't be good for you. Give me a coffee instead, black."

Gloria laughs. "Okay, coming right up."

"Oh, Gloria, would you mind asking Jack to come chat with me if he has a moment, please?"

"Sure thing." She heads to the back.

Victoria pops into my mind. I wonder if she'd like this place, and make a mental note to take her here sometime. Then berate myself for even assuming she wants to see me again. I've always been a bit too hopeful.

A few minutes later Jack's large physique appears beside me, holding two cups of coffee. "Did you get lost on your way to Debbie's or something?" His voice is deep and oozes sarcasm.

"Hey, Jack. How've you been?"

"Good." He sits. "Business has been good these summer months thanks to the tourists, and they tip my waitresses well, so it leaves them happy campers. We all win. What's new with you? New case got you stumped?"

"How'd you know?"

Jack shrugs. "You tend to come here asking if there's any word on the street when a case stumps you, Rich. Now what's the case?"

I laugh. "I guess you're right. You are my go-to when I need a little help, and I appreciate it." I wring my hands together. "The case is about a missing teenage girl. Cops suspect she's a runaway, but the family thinks otherwise. I'm leaning on the side of the family. Have you heard of any missing teenagers lately?"

"No, I can't say that I have, but I'll keep my ears open and give you a call if I hear anything."

"Thanks, Jack."

"Here, try the coffee. I'm testing out a new brand, and I'm not sure about it."

I take a sip. The coffee is dark, but not too bitter with a touch of a nutty tone. "I like it. It's a keeper."

"Not too dark for ya?"

"Too dark? How's that possible? Who doesn't like their coffee dark? People who shouldn't be trusted, that's who."

Jack roars with laughter. "You got that right." He takes down the last of his coffee. "You're right. It's good." He gets up from the table. "The breakfast rush will get here soon. Gotta get back to the grill. See ya around, Rich."

"See ya, Jack."

His not knowing about any missing teens is good, since it meant there were not any notable kidnappings in this local area, but it has me worried for Julie. Where could she be?

"Here ya go, pancakes, bacon and hash browns." She refills my cup. "Is there anything else I can getcha?"

"I'm good, Gloria. Thanks!"

"Okay, call me if you need anything." She heads off to fill more coffee cups and I dig into the plate of food. Jack's pancakes are almost as good as Debbie's burgers. Fluffy pancakes and crispy bacon with perfectly cooked hash browns. I smother it all in maple syrup and it's gone in no time. Gloria brings me the check with a smile. "Don't be a stranger now. Come back soon."

"I will. Thanks." I leave her enough cash to cover the bill and a sizable tip, then head out to start the day.

It's still early, but the heat is already creeping into the nineties and the sun's beating down on me. It will be another hot one, and I am glad the office has air.

Amanda's desk is empty when I get there. I open the doors for business and settle in for the long day on the case.

When Amanda shows up ten minutes later, I'm staring blankly at the board. "Boss, you will not believe what I've found. There has been talk on the street of a new drug lord in town, a powerful man no one's seen but everyone's heard of."

"How's that possible? I thought all the drug lords had their hands on a territory and don't let their paths cross?"

"That's usually true. This guy's bulldozed on in and does what he wants. There's been a rise in gang violence and murders. We've all seen the news, but what we haven't heard is the reason why. This boss is the reason and he appears untouchable. Sounds like he lines the pockets of most of the force, more so than any others in town."

"What does this mean for our case?"

"Let me get to that, Rich. Be patient and let me finish my story." She takes a breath. "So I found out he's been able to work his way into town due to his low prices. His price is like half that of all the others. Word on the street is he's supplementing his income with other business, including working girls."

She punches her fist in the air. "It boils my blood to hear of a pimp intimidating young girls and ruining their lives. My sources say there's an area of town with a few apartment rentals where they say the action's going down. Place seems to be guarded by gang members and any questions into it causes trouble, so my guys don't know much more. Their clients are not the ones seeking this kind of pleasure, if you know what I mean. The whole thing is pretty hush hush."

She paces the room and I wait for her to finish. "Seems to me the guys found a whole new set of clientele and most of them pay a whole lot better than the ones I'm used to." Her eyes are bloodshot and staring at me.

"Did you get any sleep, Amanda?"

"Don't worry about me, Rich. Listen to what I'm saying. I think our girl was taken, or coaxed, into this ring of thugs and now she may be part of a sex ring for prominent business men – sick ones."

"That's crazy. You'd think that sort of thing would have gotten around by now and we would have heard something. The cops would have taken it down."

"Rich, you know as well as I that a large chunk of the cops in this town are corrupt as hell. It'd be easy to cover this up. Especially if they're getting paid very well for their allegiance."

"Yeah, but this is pretty bad, even for them."

"I'm telling you, Rich. This is the word on the street, and you know my sources are good."

I've been working with Amanda long enough to know that when she gets a feeling, I need to listen. "Okay. I'll think it over. Get me the info on the area your guys say this is going down."

"Sure thing." She heads to her desk.

"And Amanda..."

"Yeah, boss?"

"You should go home and get some sleep."

"No. I'm too pissed to sleep. I need to work. I'll sleep tonight."

"Promise?"

"Promise. You worry too much, Rich. I'm good." She shuts the door behind her.

I write her theory on a card and tape in on the board. The story seems crazy but when Amanda gets this way I've learned to go with it. Often she's right, and when she's wrong, she's not too far off. There must be something to the story. I just hope it's not our girl.

And I don't want to believe my fellow boys on the force can stoop that low.

Chapter Seven

An hour later I haven't moved, and still have no idea where to start, when Amanda walks in. "Boss, here is a map of the city with the area I told you about highlighted. Also you have a meeting with Carl, his wife, and daughter in twenty minutes, so you should head out. You were going there, right?"

"Oh, right. Thanks. I wasn't watching the clock." I grab a Mt. Dew from my mini fridge. "Want one?"

"Nope. Sugar will have me climbing the walls. You shouldn't drink that stuff."

"I know, but it tastes so good. I'm headed out. Hold down the fort for me."

Outside is even hotter than yesterday, so I hail a cab.

Carl lets me in when I get to their house, which is only a few blocks from my mother's. Florence and Glenda look as though they've gotten no sleep and haven't stopped crying for days.

"Thank you for seeing me. I know it's a bad time, but I want to get every bit of information I can get from you. It all helps."

Carl speaks. "Anything you need, Mr. Stryker."

"Rich, please call me Rich. First thing, do you have a recent picture of Julie?"

Florence hands me a photo. "This one is from a few months ago." She holds in a sob. "Her hair is a bit longer but..." She puts her face in her hands and cries.

Glenda finishes for her. "She recently dyed her hair a deep shade of purple, but otherwise she looks the same." She turns to console her daughter.

"Thank you." I've never been comfortable with crying, so I don't know what else to say.

Carl hands me sheets of lined paper covered with small writing. "We came up with a list of all her friends from the past two years, and everything we could remember about them. There is also a list of places she liked to visit, going as far back as we can remember. We also listed names and addresses of relatives and anyone we could think of who may know anything about her. It's all there, but if you need anything else we will be happy to get it for you."

"I have one last request, and it may seem like an intrusion, but it can also give me insight into the case. Would you mind if I check out her room? Of course you can say no, or stay with me the whole time if you'd like, but having a look will give me a feel for her personality."

Glenda looks up and I can't read her expression. Is she angry or hopeful? "Of course. You do what you gotta do. Carl will show you the way, and you take your time. We trust you."

"Thank you, ma'am."

I follow Carl up the stairs to a small corner bedroom. The room shows signs of a young, lively girl transformed into a dark, brooding teenager. The walls are a vibrant pink, but hanging on them are pictures of metal bands and drawings of dark, eerie scenes.

"I'll be downstairs if you need anything." Carl leaves me and I get to work.

First, I stand in the middle of the room and take it all in, and then I search for the obvious hiding spots for all young girls; under the bed, in her dresser drawers, and others but come up empty. Then I search the closet and find a small box in the corner under a pair of dress shoes.

The box contains an e-cigarette, a half-smoked joint and a small, empty bottle of Jack Daniel's. I'm glad I don't find any hard drugs like meth or heroin, and put the box back where I find it.

A search of the rest of the closet comes up empty. I'm disappointed to find no journal, but not completely surprised. Most girls don't take up that hobby anymore.

On her desk, I find a few pictures of Julie and some friends. Happy girls, smiling and dressed up ready for a dance I assume. They must be her old friends. I make a mental note to call them.

There is also a folded piece of paper on her desk. The need to know what it says, overcomes my need to uphold Julie's privacy. The note reads:

Julie Babe—I'm so glad we met. I love you and want to be with you. Who cares what your family says. People are idiots anyways. Think about what I said. Friday is the day. I'll be waiting. –Emillio

Bingo. This is huge. It appears as though she was pressured to leave her family or at least someone tried to talk her into it. Now the question is whether she did actually run away or was she taken?

Back downstairs I grab the pictures and papers the family gave me and decide to leave. I do not want to prolong the sorrow. Besides, Carl told me a majority of the story yesterday, and I have enough to move forward.

"Thank you very much for taking the time to get me all this information. It will help a lot. I promise I will do what I can to get your daughter back safe and sound."

"We know you will. Thank you." Glenda's eyes are filled with hope.

"Thank you so much for helping us." Florence wraps me up in a hug and starts to cry again.

I pat her back. "I will not let you down."

She gives me a squeeze, then let's go.

I'm not sure why I said those words. I was compelled to end her sorrow and they just came out. The bar I am setting for myself is getting a little too high.

Carl takes my hand. "Thank you, Rich, and please call if you need anything else."

"Will do." I hurry out the door, needing to get away from all the sadness in the room, and hope aimed at me.

My mother usually has Tuesday mornings off, so I head to her place for lunch. She's sitting in front of the TV watching *Young and the Restless* when I walk in the living room.

"What you doing here Rich? Not that I'm not glad to see you, sweetheart."

"I was in the area visiting the Nelsons and thought I'd swing by."

"That poor family. I can't imagine all the worry they are going through, not knowing where their little girl has gone. You are a bright light in their cloud of darkness, honey. Thank you for helping them."

The need to make my mom proud stops me from telling her how little information I have to handle the case. "You still watch this, mom? Isn't it the same thing over and over? Someone dies, then comes back to life, another cheats or gets kidnapped, not once, but twice? Always the same."

She slaps my arm. "It's not all the same and don't give me crap about my TV shows."

I laugh. "Want me to make you lunch?"

"No, sweetheart. We both know how well you cook. Let me take out some leftover lasagna to heat up."

"Yum, lucky me!" Her lasagna is my favorite. I follow her into the kitchen.

"So tell me about the case."

"You know I can't do that mom. The cases are confidential and I can't go around telling people about them."

"I know, but I figured maybe I could help you hash it out, help lead you down the right path."

"Don't worry about me. I've got leads and sources out there. I will figure this out, okay?"

"Okay, okay."

She drops the topic and for the rest of our lunch, she fills the conversation with gossip about all her crazy neighbors.

It seems there are always new people moving in as others leave, and my mom keeps tabs on all of them – she and the three other ladies she calls 'her girls.' They get together at least twice a week to play cards and 'talk' as she calls it. My mom lives for these nights.

Since I left the house for the academy, she had to busy herself with something interesting. The girls fill that spot. They are a lovely bunch of women, and the four of them keep the neighborhood on its toes. The neighbors keep getting younger though, and poorer, but the women still take it upon themselves to yell at anyone getting too rowdy, or help a mom in need of a moment to herself.

Sometimes I worry for her safety, but for the most part everyone is good to them, and knows them as the neighborhood angels – always there to help you out and set you straight. Still, the security system alleviates my worries at night.

When noon rolls around my mom gets ready for work, and she leaves in the Toyota I bought her a few years back. When she works nights at the library I worry, and I don't like her walking or taking the bus, so getting her a car was the best option. At first, she resisted, but now she loves that car and takes it everywhere.

I keep telling her she can quit her job completely. I'd pay the bills, but she won't hear of it. Mom says she needs to be a functioning part of the world and do something useful. Plus she loves her job, so I let it go.

Even though it's hot as hell, I walk back to work.

Chapter Eight

Back at the office, I make some calls. The list the Nelsons gave me is thorough, but I need to hear from her old friends.

The story is the same from all three girls. They had been close, but a few months ago Julie started to hang out with this new boy, Emillio, and his gang of friends.

None of the girls liked him and told Julie, but she wouldn't listen and instead started to push them way. Eventually, she stopped hanging out with the three girls. They were certain Emillio was the reason for Julie's disappearance.

All three also told me they thought Emillio was in a gang. They explained that he and his friends always wore the same colored clothes: black, blue, and white.

An internet search pulls up a known gang of Chicago, the Royals, who wore the black, blue and white colors the girls spoke of on the phone.

Now all I need to do is find out if she left voluntarily or was she taken. How am I going to find that out?

My phone rings.

"Rich speaking."

"Hey Rich, it's John and have I got a story for you. I looked into the reported missing girl cases in the past six months and noticed a pattern. They started to increase dramatically in number about four months ago. Also, they seem to be concentrated in the Englewood, Washington Park, and Greater Grand Crossing areas. They are all from single-family homes and most of them are young girls."

"But Anderson..."

"I know what you are about to say, but let me get to the good stuff. They are all typical cases, but what I found to be a vague connection is each of the girls had started to hang out with a new group of friends. The parents express concern about the new friends, but that was all the info I could find."

He sighs, "I fear the girls are being targeted because of their vulnerability, and then drawn in and eventually convinced to run away. Or they get kidnapped. I truly worry what happens to them after they are taken. This may run deep, Rich. You sure you want to get involved in this?"

"I do. I found out that our girl became friends with a group from what looks to be the Royals gang, probably the same group as the rest of the girls. Amanda has a theory they are being used for sex slavery, and if that's the case, I need to get them out."

"Amanda's not wrong very often."

"I know."

"Well, I'm here for you. I will do what I can, but we'll have to be careful. This one feels corrupt and if I dig too much, I may spook the wrong person and lose us any chance of finding the girl."

"I understand. Thanks for all your help, John. I appreciate it."

"Talk to you later, Rich."

"Bye."

This is not looking good. John's info is similar to Amanda's, and I don't like it.

Amanda bursts into my office. "Okay. Here's a map of Chicago. I have highlighted the area my sources say the brothel is located in blue. I highlighted all the reported missing cases in pink and the unreported cases in green."

She tapes the map to the center of the whiteboard.

"Thanks, Amanda. John thinks the girls are befriended by a new group of kids, same as Julie. I think they are part of the Royals gang and they do it strategically."

"The Royals, huh? They have sort of been a background gang for years. Makes sense that the new boss would align with a small gang he can easily control. I'll check into it."

"Thanks!"

The phone rings.

"Hello, Rich speaking."

"Rich, it's Victoria."

"Oh, hi." I'm at a loss for words, as usual.

"I had fun yesterday."

"Me too." More silence.

"Rich, I was wondering if you were busy tonight."

"Uhm, not really."

"Okay, well then......would you want to go do something?"

"Sure." I rack my brain for ideas. "I know they have a concert in the park at Washington tonight. Would you like to check it out?"

"Sounds wonderful."

"How about I meet you at the same spot at five-thirty again?"

"Sounds like a plan. I'll see you then."

I hang up and study the map on the board. So many girls not found and all of them from higher crime parts of town.

Somebody did their homework and is trying hard to make this appear like random runaways so the cops won't search too deeply into it. My mind wanders to old Benny. Cops like him are known to be corrupt and willing to do almost anything for the right amount of payback, but even this seems low for him. What kind of horrid person do you have to be to get into this business, or even turn a blind eye as it happens?

But then again, Benny is a pretty terrible person himself. I disliked him from the first day we met when he threatened me over a parking spot. He was a complete arrogant prick and oozed a hideous amount of sleaze. He never liked me much either. I was too book-smart for him to assume I could ever be a good enough cop with street smarts.

We learned to tolerate each other until the night he beat his high school sweetheart wife close to death. The beating landed her in the hospital and she lost their unborn child. Charges were dropped, of course. He claimed she fell down the stairs, but I knew better. From then on I gave him as much crap as he dished out and it pissed him off to no end.

There are other cops on the force like him, but I try to think most of the guys are fairly decent. The ones that do go corrupt are either blackmailed into it or are offered enough money that they can't say no.

I witnessed too many good cops turn sour in my days on the force. No matter how hard I tried to talk them out of it, they always stayed in and would push me away. Eventually I couldn't watch it anymore, and feared I'd get sucked in, so I left.

Most of the corruption started out small – look the other way on this drug deal and we'll slip you a share of the dough. But it's snowballed into so much more since the early days – don't look too hard into this murder or your family could be next.

Stuff that shouldn't happen but it does, so I should not be surprised if it comes to this, cops looking the other way on sex trafficking. The thought of it makes me sick to my stomach.

I shake my head. If this is true, I need to get to the bottom of this quickly. Julie is running out of time. All these girls need my help.

The map taunts me, daring me to figure it all out, but revealing very little.

I decide to do online research of the apartment complexes in the area Amanda highlighted for a possible home base center for trafficking.

It's tedious work, but my search comes up with two possibilities. Most of the buildings show typical rental activity, but these two show vague ads about short term rentals with no real information.

Hope shoots through me. My eagerness to go out and check the buildings right now burns inside.

I pull out a Twinkie from my drawer and press the intercom button. "Amanda, you interested in a little field trip?"

"You read my mind, boss. Let's go."

Chapter Nine

I grab a Mt. Dew for me and water for Amanda from my little fridge and meet Amanda outside my office. "Let's get my car and head out."

Along the way Amanda describes the different gangs in the area. Each has its own dress code and territory in town. There are more gangs than I remember and I'm glad she knows her stuff.

I hold my breath as we near the first building. We drive in circles around it several times and nothing jumps out at us, so Amanda suggests we go to the second building and check it out.

As usual, the streets of Chicago are busy, so our first pass gives us nothing. The second time around Amanda spots a small group of boys wearing the Royal colors.

"You see 'em, boss?"

"I do."

"What do you want to do? Keep driving or get out and walk?"

"That depends, how heroic do you feel, Amanda?"

"I'm thinking our girls need a hero. Let's go."

I pay for parking and we head for the building.

"So, boss. What's the plan?"

"We are a couple looking for an apartment and we want to check out the place. Follow my lead." I take her hand. "You doing okay?"

"I'm good, boss, real good. Don't worry about me."

We slow as we get closer to the group of gang members near the building and pretend interest.

"Looks nice, honey." Amanda says as she strokes my arm. "Let's go inside."

"Sure thing, beautiful." I lead her to the front door.

"Hey man, what you doing?" the largest of the boys asks me.

"My wife and I are looking for an apartment and this building piqued our interest, so she wants to check it out. May I ask why that's your business?"

"You want to back off, man. This is our building and there are no apartments for rent, so fuck off."

Amanda steps forward. "I doubt this is your building, and the ad on the internet says otherwise."

"Lady, you're about to piss me off and that ain't never good. So turn around and walk your happy ass back where you came from."

I grab her arm to hold her back. "Let's go, honey. We don't want to deal with this. It's best if we leave."

"Yeah, honey. Listen to your boy." Another of the boys adds as I pull Amanda away.

Two blocks away, she stops. "Why did we leave? It's not like you to wimp out."

"I got all the info I needed. Plus it's too early in the game to pick a fight and give ourselves away. We need a plan to get Julie and all those other girls out if, in fact, they are in that building. Okay?"

She huffs. "Fine, but promise me we will come back and do something." Her eyes plead with me.

"I promise. We're going to get them out."

"Okay."

We head back to the car.

"Boss, can we do a few loops around the neighborhoods the girls are being taken from?"

"Sure thing, but I've got to get the map from the office."

"Boss, you forget. I've got it all here." She taps her head.

"Right, then let's go."

It has been years since I've been in some of the neighborhoods, and parts are not looking too hot. Rundown houses, some of them completely boarded up, and trash strewn all over the streets.

Many houses have people hanging out on the lawns and porches. In a few neighborhoods we find groups of teens wearing the Royal colors.

"Boss, I think our theory of the gang befriending these girls may be true. It's looking as though it's not as far-fetched as it first seemed."

"I think you're right, Amanda. Let's go figure out what to do next."

Fifteen minutes later, we're staring at the whiteboard in my office.

"Okay, boss. What we know so far is that girls around these neighborhoods are being befriended by a new group of kids, and then go missing." She points to the pink and green highlighted areas of the city.

"The building we checked out does appear to be a part of something shady, as we saw ourselves." She points to the new index card full of the information we learned on our little drive. "Now what do we do?"

I take it all in, studying the board. Wanting something to pop out at me, something to become clear.

"Why don't we just go blazing in there with John and light it up?"

"We can't do that, Amanda. I will not risk getting you or John hurt, or even worse, killed."

"We'll be fine, Rich. We need to help these girls."

"We will Amanda, we will, but we can't be crazy about it."

"Then how?"

"I need to check out one more thing tonight and then we will go in. I promise."

"What are you gonna check, Rich? I can help."

"It's nothing you can help with. I got this, I will do this and have a plan by tomorrow. It's almost five now. How about you go home and get some rest. Tomorrow will be a busy day."

She hesitates.

"Go. We will get them. Trust me, Amanda. Have I ever let you down?"

"Fine, but tomorrow we do something. Right?"

"Promise."

She heads for the door then turns to face me. "Rich, I know I'm pushing hard on this one, but it's hitting too close to home."

"I know. I've got your back...always."

"Thanks." She gives me a weak smile and leaves.

I study the board a few more minutes before I leave.

The plan for tonight is a crazy one, but I have to do it. I have to be sure.

Chapter Ten

On the way to pick up Victoria, I stop into a corner market and pick up a few essentials; wine, cheese, bread, sausage, grapes and olives.

Victoria is waiting on the bench when I get to the university. "Sorry to keep you waiting."

"I just got here, so don't worry. What you got there?" Her hand flies to her mouth. "Sorry, I'm being nosy. I tend to talk sometimes without thinking."

I laugh at her adorable honesty. "Not nosy. Curious. It's our picnic dinner. It's what people do during these concerts."

"Sounds wonderful! Thanks!"

"Shall we go?" I instinctively hold out my hand.

She easily takes it with a smile. "Let's go."

We walk the few blocks to Washington Park. The band is setting up when we get there, so we walk around the park.

"So how was your day?" I ask to break the silence

"Good. I'm almost ready to start teaching and my office is pretty much put together. It was a productive day."

"That's good. When does school start again?"

"A little over a week from now."

"I'm sure you'll do awesome! The kids are lucky to have you as a teacher."

She beams at me. "Thanks! I hope so. How was your day?"

"It was fine." I'm ready to take my mind off the missing girls. "Want to sit? The music should start soon."

"Sounds good."

We find a spot near the stage.

"I forgot to bring a blanket, but they had larger towels at the store, so I hope they work."

She laughs. "It'll be great I don't mind the grass or bugs."

This woman keeps getting better and better. "Good." I pull out all the goodies and soon we the hear music start.

This time it's a jazz band and their sound is incredible. They play a good mix of up-beat and slow songs. The wine and food is tasty, and my company is even better.

Victoria smiles and claps to the songs. Every once in a while she makes a comment about how much fun she's having or how great the music sounds. Her obvious delight brightens my dark day and I forget about the case for a while.

An hour in, a slower song starts and a few couples get up to dance. Even more people take up the idea and Victoria watches them with envy.

"Would you like to dance?" I am not a dancer, but the need to please her runs high.

"I'd love to."

I take her hand and pull her close. We start to waltz. The only dance I know. It's still hot outside, but neither of us is bothered by the extra body heat.

She smiles up at me as we dance. The beat gives way to an even slower song. It's not the right beat for the waltz, but I'm not ready to let her go just yet, so I pull her closer and sway to the music. She rests her head on my chest and wraps her arms around my waist. When the song ends, I reluctantly let her go.

"That was nice." Victoria's face is inches from mine. Her breath tickles my lips.

It clouds my thinking and I lean in to press my mouth to hers. She kisses me back and parts her lips to let my tongue slip in.

My body urges me to pull her close and touch her everywhere, but I control myself and enjoy the tenderness of the moment. I cup her face in my hands and caress her lips with mine again before pulling away.

"I liked that even more." Her grin says it all.

"I agree." I notice movement in the corner of my eye and find the band has stopped playing and people are packing up their things to go. "I guess the band is done."

My watch says eight. I don't want the night to end. "Did you want to go grab a drink?"

"That sounds great."

We pack up our picnic. Victoria grabs my hand and we head off to a small corner bar a few blocks away.

Many people have the same idea, so the place is packed. We manage to find a couple of stools at the far end of the bar.

"What would you like to drink?"

"I'll just take a beer."

I order two Miller Lite tap beers and we drink them in silence. I'm not sure what to say. I'm not a talker.

"So, Rich, you seem drained today. What's stressing you out? Not me, I hope."

"No, not you at all. You're the bright part of my day."

She beams. "That's good to hear." Her look turns serious. "Want to talk about it?"

"I'm good. I don't want to burden or worry you. It's just the case. I'm at a troubling point and not sure where to go from here."

"You won't burden me. Sometimes an outside opinion can help. I'm here if you need me."

Her look invites me in and before I know it I've told her the outline of the case.

Her face falls as I describe the details. "Wow. That's pretty intense. This seems like a complex case." She pauses and looks up as if in thought. "I will say that from my side of it, the idea of prominent men seeking out that type of illegal behavior is not that crazy. Men in power seek out more ways than one to show that power." She hesitates. "As far as your fellow police officers go, when people get a little power, they tend to want to keep it and protect it. So it would not be too far out of the realm of what they may be willing to do."

"Those are my exact fears. I don't want to think the worst of people, but all the signs point in that direction." I take her hands in mine. "Thanks for listening."

"Anytime, it's always good to talk things out."

We talk for another hour about her new job and a few of the other places she wants to see in Chicago before I walk her home at ten.

I stop at her door. Once more in that awkward what-to-do position. She gazes up at me and I take the risk and move in for the kiss.

My lips caress hers and she kisses back with passion. I pull her into my arms and the chemistry between us heats up. My mouth melts into hers and I don't want to stop. My hands want to explore her, but I resist and try to maintain my composure. I reluctantly pull away an almost stumble off the stairs.

Victoria smiles. "I had a great time, Rich."

"Me too. Can I call you tomorrow?"

"Please do."

I kiss her gently one more time. "Good night, Victoria."

"Good night, Rich."

I walk away, realizing I forgot my car at work. The walk to the office is quick, but along the way I've made up my mind to stick to my crazy plan.

Chapter Eleven

The roads are less congested along the way since it is so late, but the streets around the apartment building are busy with people.

I take two laps around with my car, but don't get as good of a glimpse as I'd like, so I park my car and get out to walk.

There are the usual crowds of rowdy kids and loud adults huddled in groups along the street, but as I get closer to the building I notice lone girls quietly working the streets, older girls, around eighteen. They approach the men walking near the building. Some men stop to talk, while others keep walking.

More than half the men approach the group of boys guarding the same door Amanda and I tried to enter earlier. The boys appear to ask questions before letting the men walk through.

I stupidly decide to try my luck again, since it's a different group of boys and head for the door.

"Whoa, dude. Where you think you're going?"

"I'm joining in on the fun, boys."

"Oh, really? Tell me who sent you."

"The man. The boss. You know."

The leader of the group scoffs at me and glances toward his friend. "No, I don't know. Who is this boss man you talk about?"

"I'm here for the girls, so just let me in."

That was clearly the wrong thing to say.

"I don't think you understand how this works." The leader stands up and cracks his knuckles. "We don't know nothing about no girls and it's time for you to go. Here let me help you."

He grabs for my arm, but my instincts kick in and I grab his instead and pull him in to elbow him straight in the nose. I hear a loud crack and he goes down to the ground.

At first his group of friends stand in shock, before a few of them realize what happened and move forward towards me.

I hoped it would not come to this. "You don't want to do this."

Two of them give each other looks, then one lunges for my head and the other for my chest.

I manage to jump towards the third and sidekick him in the neck as the other two smack into each other. I bang their heads together for good measure.

Three down. How many more to go? I glance around. Two left, they stare at me but don't move. "I was only here for fun, boys. Now you can either let me walk away or end up like these four. What's it gonna be?"

They exchange looks and glance away.

I haul ass back to my car. A few other groups eye me up along the way, but none come near me.

Once in my car, I waste no time getting the hell out of there. I know what needs to be done. This ends tomorrow and no one's going to stop me.

No one.

I forgo heading home and head back to the office to make a late night call.

"Hello."

"John, sorry if I woke you, but I need your help."

I tell him my plan and what I need him to do, then set out to plan the details of my take-down.

Around three A.M., I finally mapped out everything and decide to crash on the couch in my office.

"WAKE UP, RICH."

I feel a nudge on my shoulder.

"Rich, wake up."

I realize it's Amanda and sit up quickly. "Amanda, I have a plan."

"Whoa, wait, boss. What?"

"I went back to the apartment last night and just about got my ass kicked, but now my gut says those girls are inside and we need to get them out of there." I get up and pull a Mt. Dew out of the fridge. I'm going to need the energy today. "I have a plan to get Julie out and, if everything goes well, those other girls, too."

"That was very dangerous, Rich."

"Don't lecture me, Amanda. I had to be sure. Now I am and we need to move fast."

Just then good old Benny Hartman bursts into my office.

"Hello, Dick. We need to talk...get out, Amanda."

"You have no right to talk to me like that, Benjamin."

"Get out, whore. I need to have a word with Mr. Dick Tracy himself and you need to see your way out."

Amanda starts to get up in his face, but I want to get this over with and get him out. "I got this, Amanda. Please take this and make a copy." I hand her the sheet with my notes.

She shoots me a look of death, but grabs the paper and storms out.

"Yeah, bitch, get going."

I've had it. I cold-cock him alongside his face as he turns back to me and he falls to the floor.

Amanda smiles and keeps walking. "Yeah, keep talking, asshole. You're not in the precinct anymore."

Benny scrambles to his feet. "What the fuck!" He comes at me, but I'm ready. I front kick him in his precious jewels. Then round kick him on the side of the head to knock him on the floor.

I climb on top of him and grab both of his ears and pull his face to mine. "Don't talk to my assistant like that, got it? I don't care for it. Now, why are you here, uninvited?" I throw his head to the floor and jump up off of him.

He slowly raises himself off the ground and shakes off the kicks, then coughs a few times. When he speaks his voice is strained. "I don't care for you looking into my cases, Dick."

"My name is Rich, and what case are you referring to?"

"You know damn well what I mean. You have been snooping into the missing Nelson girl case, and it's none of your business."

"Oh, right. Well, Benny boy, it looks as though the family has little faith in your ability to find their missing daughter. They came to me, hoping I'd do a better job of finding her."

That comment hits Benny hard and he lunges for me, but I grab his arm and get behind him in an arm lock.

"Get off me, asshole."

"Now, now, Benny. As soon as you can behave rationally like an adult, I'll let you go. You've already felt what I can do to you so you may want to play nice." I squeeze his arm back and up, adding to his pain. "You ready to be a good boy now?"

"Fine! Just let me the fuck go!"

I shove him away from me. "I'm pretty sure you're here because I've been looking into a few things you don't want me to uncover, and your boss man is on your ass to get rid of me. Well too bad for you, Benny boy. I'm not going anywhere, so you can go let your crooked boss and partners know I'm coming for your ass. Now get out of my office and never show your face here again." I stare him down.

He hesitates. This is not my usual demeanor, and it's an obvious shock.

"Beat it." I'm pissed and so ready to go all out on him after all these years of tolerating his ass.

He backs out of my office.

"And make sure you apologize to Amanda on your way out or I'll make sure you pay, Benny. I mean it."

He bumps into the frame, then turns around and leaves.

I hear a muffled 'sorry' before the door to our office slams shut.

Amanda appears in my office. "Thanks, Rich." Her face wears pure joy.

"No problem. He's an ass, and no one should ever be allowed to talk to you like that, Amanda."

"You're a good man." She hands me a sheet of paper. "Here's your copy. Some hell of a plan you have there. Think it'll work?"

"I do." I focus on her. "It has to."

"It could be dangerous for you, and how come I'm sitting on the sidelines?"

"You're not on the sidelines. You're my getaway car. If you don't do your job right, Julie and I are screwed. Now let's go over the plan, and then call John. I have to make sure he's good to go on his end."

Chapter Twelve

Two Mt. Dews and four Twinkies later, we are ready to go.

Amanda takes the driver's seat and I'm shotgun. She heads for the apartment building. There's no turning back now.

I keep one suit in my office for emergencies. This is one of those emergencies. I have to look the part I'm about to play if I get caught or things will go downhill and I'll get spotted.

Amanda insisted on adding a few finishing touches with some slicked back hair and bronzer to the face, telling me it helps disguise my appearance even more. I feel as though I'm ready for a Broadway show, but let her have her way. She may be right and I don't want to risk being recognized.

Amanda's gun is in her pocket. I don't even like it being in my car, but she wouldn't leave without it. I have never been a fan of guns. They hurt more than they help, and my goal is to get in and out quietly. Guns are not quiet.

She drops me off a block north of the building. "Be safe, Rich."

"I will." I smile at her. "This is when I'm at my best. Don't worry about me. Worry about the other guys, and be ready for my text."

"Can't I convince you to take my gun?"

"I'm good. I've got my keychain. It's all I need." I pull out the six-inch-long, half-inch-around, chiseled stick attached to a keychain hook. It's my weapon of choice from the dojo – small enough to carry it in your pocket, yet a highly-effective instrument of pain if used in the correct way.

"That little thing? I've got pocket knives bigger than that."

I chuckle. "It's all I need, and size isn't everything. Now get going. I've got some rescuing to do."

She pulls the car away and I take off toward the building.

My search of the building yesterday revealed two options: the front door, which is impossible for me at this point, or the fire escape. So fire escape it is, but it's higher than it looked from the road.

The jump will be tough in this suit and dress shoes, but I go for it. I sprint and throw myself towards the lowest rung, lucky to catch it with my right hand, but almost slip off as my momentum carries me forward. I swing back and reach to grab it with my left hand.

Lifting weights pays off as I pull my body up the rungs one by one till I can reach the lowest rung with my feet to crawl up the rest of the way to the second floor. I take the stairs to the third floor.

My bet is the first and second floors are busy with all kinds of action and the top floors are where they let the businessmen take their rented company, so the middle floors are where I want to start. It's my safest bet.

My bad luck is at it again when I discover the window is locked. I peer in and find no one in the hallway.

A locked window will not hold me back, so I pull out my keychain and cover the end with my suit fabric. The squares of the window are small, so I hope the sound of the breaking glass won't be too loud.

I give the pane one good smack and the cracking sound is so loud I swear the whole gang of thugs will come running to get me, so I pull back and hide.

A few minutes later I sneak a peek through the windows, but see no one in the hallway. Maybe it was not as bad as I thought. I clear the broken shards of glass from the pane before I get my hand through to unlock the window and push it open. Still, I see no one, so I climb in and try to open the first door.

It opens, but the place is empty, so I move onto the next. Each apartment down the line is as empty as the last till I reach the end.

Maybe I was wrong.

Do I move on to the fourth floor or go down to the second?

My gut instinct says fourth, but after no luck on this floor my head says the reasonable choice would be to go down to the second. After an internal struggle, I go with my gut and head up the stairs.

I reach the top and peer out the window to the hall. It is clear, so I open the door. A few steps from the first door I hear the ping of the elevator.

Panic sets in. I try for the knob but it's locked. Crap. Without thinking I head for the next door, and realize I should have headed back to the stairwell, but it may be too late.

The handle on the second door sticks slightly, but then turns and opens. I run in and shut it behind me.

A whimper causes me to turn.

On the couch in the living room sits a petite girl, only about thirteen years old. She is tilted over the arm of the couch with her head back.

I glance around the room, but find no one else.

The girl's legs are tied together at the ankles so I rush over to help her. "I'm here. I'll untie your ankles."

There's no response. Only a moan. I open her eyes. They are blood shot and unresponsive. That's when I notice the needle marks on her arms. What do they have her on?

I hear the knob turn and muffled voices behind the door. Do I leave her and keep going on my mission, or help her and risk it all? I make up my mind and hide behind the wall leading to the kitchen.

The men walk up to the girl. "Wake-up sunsh..." Smack.

I hit the first guy in the temple with my keychain and he goes down. He is still alive, barely, though he'll wake up with a severe headache.

The second guy responds quicker than I anticipate and punches me in the gut. It slows me down, but I recover and ridge hand him in the neck. His hands instinctively reach for his throat and I push him onto the couch, giving him and elbow to the face. He passes out.

The girl is so out of it she doesn't even move. I know I can't take her with me so I tell myself I've done enough for now and leave for the next apartment.

This one contains six more girls, all passed out. Julie isn't among them, but all are faces I recognize from the printouts.

These bastards need to pay. I reluctantly leave the girls behind and move on. I find more girls in the next three apartments, but still no sign of Julie.

I hear muffled voices from behind the door to the last apartment, but decide to move in anyway. I'm mad now and looking for a fight.

The door's unlocked, like the rest, and I barge in to find three guys slapping around a girl in a chair.

Julie. Blue hair and the same pretty face, all beat up now by her captors.

"Get your goddamn hands off her."

"Who the fuck are you?" A big guy off to the left takes a step towards me.

"I'm your worst nightmare. Now if you know what's good for you you'll get your hands off her and walk away."

The guy to the right laughs. "Is that right?" He cracks his knuckles as if to scare me.

"Yep. That's right. I already put two of you guys out of commission for a few days. Why not three more?"

They give each other looks, then all three come at me.

I grab the guy on the left and pull him into the thug in the middle as I sidekick the third in the gut. He crumples to the ground. The other two recover quickly. One punches me in the face. He gets me good and I stumble back. The other grabs my arms.

Stupid move.

I pick up my legs and swing all my weight down to the ground as I lean forward. He loses his balance and falls over my head, kicking his partner in the head, knocking him out cold.

The guy I kicked, recovers and stands up to come at me only to receive a blow to the nuts then a whack to the side of the head with the heel of my shoe.

Two down, one to go – the largest one of the three – and he's pissed. He charges for me, but I've saved my best move for last and spin kick him right in the neck. He crumples to the ground. For a minute I wonder if I kicked too hard, but a gurgled breath escapes his mouth and I exhale with relief.

I turn to Julie.

"Please don't hurt me." She's shaking with terror.

"No Julie. I'm here to save you. Your grandpa Carl sent me to find you. Let me help you out of here."

"Grandpa?"

"Yes. He was worried about you and sent me to find you. But we have to hurry. I need to get you out of here before they find me. Can you walk?"

"I...think...so." Her face is strained.

I untie her legs from the chair and help her up. She struggles to stand, probably high like the rest of the girls, and weak from the beatings.

"I've got you. Let's go." We head out of the apartment.

We are at the end of the hall by the fire escape, but there are two other guys headed my way. One pulls out a gun and takes aim, but misses by a mile. The sound is sure to get the attention of more thugs.

"Nice shot, asshole." I shouldn't piss him off, but I can't help myself.

I lean Julie against the wall. "Stay here."

I turn and run for them and throw myself on top of the first, taking him down. I punch him in the neck before the second grabs me from behind in a choke.

I reach up and yank him down over my shoulder onto the floor, then smash his chest with my fist. The weakling passes out, but I give him one more punch in the face.

The first thug tries to push himself off the floor, but I get up and kick him in the face to knock him back down for good.

We need to get out of here. There's got to be more on the way.

I open my phone and hit send, then slip it back in my pocket and grab Julie. "We have to hurry." We manage to get her out of the window and I climb out after her.

"Climb down to the second floor landing." She does as I ask without question, still in a daze.

I get to the second floor. "I'll go down first, then you come right after me and I'll catch you at the bottom."

"I'm scared."

"Don't worry. I've got you, okay?"

"Okay." She does not look convinced.

We need to move so I start down and she follows. I hit the end of the ladder and jump to the ground.

"Okay, now get to the bottom and jump. I promise I'll catch you."

"I can't! It's too far!"

"You've got this, Julie. You have to do this!"

"Come on, Julie. You have to jump!" Amanda yells from the car behind me.

There's a shuffle above us and a shot rings out. My arm swings back and I feel a sharp sting, but don't have time to care. "Let's go, Julie. It's now or never. You have to jump!"

"JUMP NOW, JULIE!" Amanda screams.

Julie lets go and I grab her and push her out of the way before a bullet bounces off the last rung. We shove into the back of the car. "Go!"

Amanda hits the gas just as the side window shatters and a bullet hits my thigh.

"Shit, what was that?"

"Just go, Amanda!"

"I'm going, boss."

We peel away as I hear sirens. Julie is crying beside me.

"It's okay, Julie. We've got you now. You're safe. Tell her, Amanda."

"Oh, sweetie. You're safe now. We're gonna take you to your mom now. Everything'll be okay." She looks at me through the rear-view mirror. "Boss, do we need to take a detour?"

I stare at my leg. It's not good. "I'm okay. Get her home." I take off my tie and wrap it around the wound, hoping to stop some of the bleeding.

We make it to the Nelsons. Amanda gets out and comes to the back. Horror fills her face when she sees the blood. "Rich! You are not okay. This is not okay. I need to get you to the hospital."

"Just get her to her family and then worry about me. I'll be fine. "

"Dammit, Rich." She grabs the still-sobbing Julie and drags her halfway up the walk before Florence, Glenda, and Carl rush out to meet her. I see Amanda gesturing and talking but can't make out what she's saying.

She rushes back and jumps into the car. "You are on your way to the hospital, and that's final."

"I'm fine. It's no big deal." And then I pass out.

Chapter Thirteen

I wake up to find myself in a hospital bed, Amanda in the seat to my left, and my mother to the right.

"Oh, thank heavens! You had me so worried, Richard. Do not ever do that again. You hear me?"

"Mom, it's not that bad."

"Not that bad?! You lost two liters of blood and they had to surgically remove a bullet from your thigh bone! But no, not bad at all. Are you crazy?"

"Well we got the girl, didn't we?"

"We sure did." Amanda beams at me.

"Richard! That does not matter right now. What matters is your life."

"Oh, mom. I'm okay. We are okay. No need to worry anymore."

"You are hopeless. I'll get the nurse."

I turn to Amanda as my mom leaves the room. "Did the plan work?"

"Like a charm." She leans toward me. "John's got connections with the DEA and convinced his guys there was a shit-ton of drugs in that apartment, but they had to move in now or it would all be gone tomorrow."

She shakes her head. "I'm not sure how he did it, but he got through to them and they came in full force with armored trucks and a helicopter. They left with three dozen guys, a ton of cash and enough drugs to supply the whole city for weeks. Plus, they got all our missing girls, and a few more on top of that."

Tears pool in her eyes. "Thank you." In all my years working with Amanda, I've never seen her cry. Not once.

"It's no big deal. It's my job."

She slaps my good leg. "It *is* a big deal. I know what they had to endure, and now they are out of there and can't be hurt anymore, thanks to you."

"Yeah, I only wish I'd gotten the boss or a few of those dirty businessmen in the process."

"Well, you'll be glad to hear there were a few clients held up in the upstairs apartments, caught with their pants down, and hopefully will pay for their sins. John says they may have also found the boss. They caught a vile old man holed up in the penthouse with a few of our missing girls. He thinks that's our guy and is hoping to get a few of the gang members to give him up for leniency."

Relief washes over me. "Good! I don't want that evil ass to be able to do this ever again."

"John says that's his goal, and he's going to make it his purpose in life to make the guy pay the price."

I relax. John never lets go of a fight. With him on the job I have no doubt the guy will pay.

Amanda slaps my hand. "And what's even better, the feds caught our good old pal Benny snorting the goods in there with our thugs. So for now he's on probation. Maybe he'll get it for this, maybe not, but it made my day to know he got caught red handed."

"Holy crap, that's awesome!"

"Yeah it is!"

Just then my mother walks back into the room. "You up for some company? The Nelsons are here."

"Julie! How's Julie?"

"She's here at the hospital, going through detox." Amanda frowns. "It looks as though she took quite a few beatings, but otherwise she was untouched. Our girl put up a fight and it may have really saved her."

"Good." I turn to my mom. "Send them in."

My mother returns with Carl and Glenda. Glenda rushes over to hug me. "Oh thank you so much for all you did, Rich! You are amazing and we owe you so much!"

"I was glad to help."

"Amanda told us you risked yourself to save our girl. We'll never be able to pay you back. Never."

"I was just doing my job. I'm glad she's back safe with you now."

"All right! Everyone out!" A nurse walks into the room. "I've got to get vitals and we need privacy, so if you would all leave for a few minutes that would be terrific."

Glenda hugs me again, "Thank you so much Mr. Stryker. Thank you!"

Carl slaps my shoulder. "I knew the moment I walked into your office you'd find our girl. Thank you, Rich, thank you!"

"You're welcome."

"Well someone's got to hold down the fort, boss. I'll be on my way. Don't take too long to heal now, you big wuss." She kisses my cheek. Another first. Then walks out.

"I'll be out in the hall, sweetheart, if you need anything. Okay, honey?"

"I'll be fine, mom. You can go home and rest. I'll be fine."

"I will do no such thing. I'll be right back." She struts out the door before I can respond.

"Let's have a look here." The nurse checks my heartbeat.

TWO DAYS LATER, I WALK out of the hospital in crutches. The bullet tore up my leg pretty good, so I'll be on them a few weeks before it's fully healed. My mother insists I stay with her for at least the first few days so she can monitor me. Moms, they never stop worrying.

The minute we get inside I reach for the phone. "Mom, I need to make a call, then I'll be in for lunch."

"Hello, University of Chicago. How may I assist you?"

"I'm trying to reach a Victoria Johnson."

"Yes, please hold and I'll direct your call." The phone rings again.

"Hello, Victoria speaking."

"Hi Victoria, It's Rich. I'm sorry I didn't call days ago, but I lost my phone and well...I was a bit incapacitated. I hope you forgive me."

"Of course, Rich. Are you okay? I saw the whole news story of the heroic rescue of those girls, but saw no mention of you, so I began to worry when you didn't call. Then Amanda found my number and told me the whole story. You are such a hero, Rich! What you put yourself through to rescue those girls was amazing."

"Thanks, but I had some help."

"Don't be modest. You deserve to be called a hero."

"Well, thanks.......I uhm......was sort of hoping we could tour the city a little more together."

"Rich, I'm not sure that would be a good idea."

My heart sinks. "Oh...okay. I understand. I..."

"No, you have it all wrong. What I mean is your leg is hurt pretty badly. You're in no shape to be walking the city."

Relief hits my chest. "True. It is a bit more difficult to get around now."

"How about I come over with a movie and popcorn? I was hoping to catch that new Jack Reacher film. You up for some company?"

I pause. "Well..."

"I'm sorry. How rude of me. Inviting myself over. Just forget what I said."

"No, that's not it at all. My mother insists I stay with her for a few days. You know moms. Always needing to tend.......if you don't mind the extra company I would love for you to come over."

Silence.

Maybe the meet the mother thing is too much and I regret letting my mom talk me into staying here.

"I would love to. I'll be over after work, around six."

I give her the address then hang up the phone. "So mom, there's

I hope you enjoyed the book!
Please consider leaving a review, it is your greatest compliment.

CHECK OUT THE NEXT book in the series!

Tom's Final Justice

CONTACT T L. ADAMS:

tamaraadamsauthor@gmail.com
www.tamaraladamsauthor.com

www.ingramcontent.com/pod-product-compliance
Lightning Source LLC
Chambersburg PA
CBHW052122150726

48002CB00006B/2452